The Adventures of Slade the Fire Dog

Stephen Boynton

Illustrations by Katie Toon

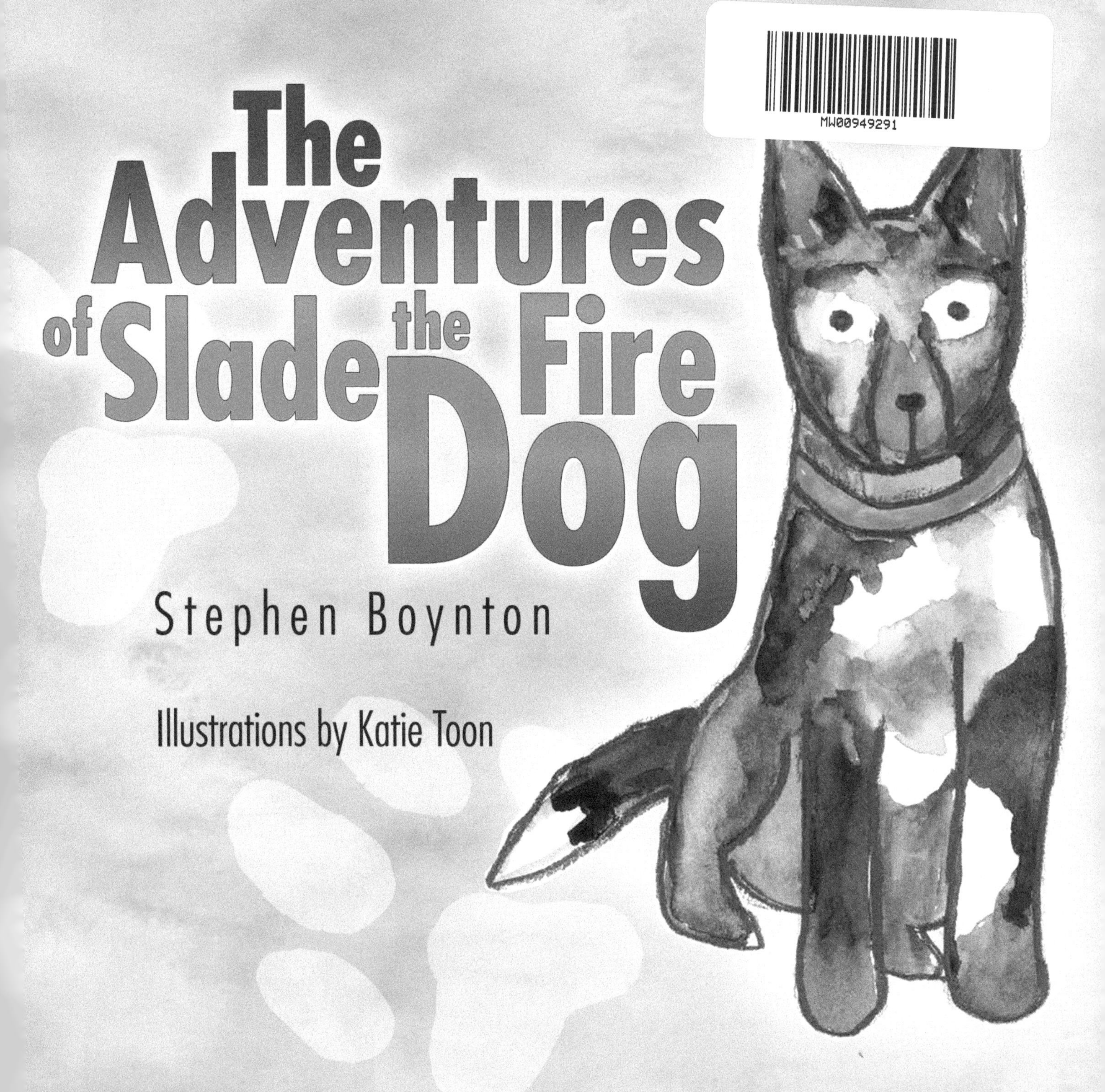

MW00949291

AuthorHouse™
1663 Liberty Drive
Bloomington, IN 47403
www.authorhouse.com
Phone: 1 (800) 839-8640

© 2018 Stephen Boynton. All rights reserved.

No part of this book may be reproduced, stored in a retrieval system,
or transmitted by any means without the written permission of the author.

Published by AuthorHouse 09/12/2018

ISBN: 978-1-5462-5875-9 (sc)
ISBN: 978-1-5462-5876-6 (e)

Library of Congress Control Number: 2018910454

Print information available on the last page.

Any people depicted in stock imagery provided by Getty Images are models,
and such images are being used for illustrative purposes only.
Certain stock imagery © Getty Images.

This book is printed on acid-free paper.

Because of the dynamic nature of the Internet, any web addresses or links contained in this book may have changed since publication and may no longer be valid. The views expressed in this work are solely those of the author and do not necessarily reflect the views of the publisher, and the publisher hereby disclaims any responsibility for them.

authorHOUSE®

This book is dedicated to my family and the Holy Spirit,
without whom this book would not have been written.

Slade lives with his Mommy.

Her name is Sharay

They go shopping for groceries together,

They go to church together,

They take vacations together.

Slade loves his mommy.

They go for walks every day. Some days they walk by the fire station. They see the fire fighters washing the fire trucks and cleaning the fire station. The fire fighters play with Slade and let him explore the station. Slade really likes the station and the fire fighters, especially Fire Fighter Stoney.

18
18

One day it rains so much there is a flood. Slade and his Mommy are in their house and the waters get too high!

The fire fighters have to come to the rescue.

They bring boats and life jackets.

Fire Fighter Stoney helps carry Slade and his Mommy to safety and everyone is OK!!

After the flood

Slade's Mommy has to move to a new place.

But there is a problem.

There is no place for Slade because they don't allow pets.

Slade is very sad.

As they are walking by the fire station one day, Slade's Mommy Sharay tells the fire fighters she is moving but can't take Slade. Fire fighter Stoney asks if Slade could stay with him and live at the fire station.

Slade has a new home.

18

Slade misses his Mommy but he is having fun in his new home. It is very big and bright. Slade helps the fire fighters wash the fire trucks and keeps the station clean and safe.

Slade has his own place to sleep downstairs at the fire station. He can't sleep upstairs with the fire fighters because he can't slide down the poles at night.

18

One day fire fighter Stoney takes Slade to the
lake for a swim. Fire fighter Stoney always wears
a life jacket when he swims. Slade remembers the
scary flood and wishes he had a life jacket too.

Slade tells Fire Fighter Stoney he wants a life jacket. Then
Slade says “We should have life jackets for all the pets”.

Fire Fighter Stoney takes the idea of
the life jackets to Chief Tom.

Chief Tom asks a local veterinarian for some
help. Dr. G tells Chief Tom they need animal life
jackets for all the fire stations in town.

Dr.G asks his friends to help him get the life jackets.

Bill and Rita offer to help.

CHIEF

One day the life jackets arrive at the station. It is a very exciting day. Dr. G comes to the fire station to visit Slade. With all the fire fighters watching, Dr. G puts a new life jacket on Slade. He proudly walks around the fire station with the new life jacket.

A newspaper photographer comes to take pictures of Slade and the new life jackets. Everybody gets in the picture.

What a great day!

That night, as fire fighter Stoney puts Slade to bed, he tells Slade “Because of your idea, the fire department can now take better care of everyone’s pets. You have helped make our community safer for all those who live here, including our four legged friends”.

Slade’s heart races as he says goodnight. Slade is so very tired but very happy too.

He goes to sleep dreaming about the wonderful things of today and wonders what great adventures tomorrow might bring.

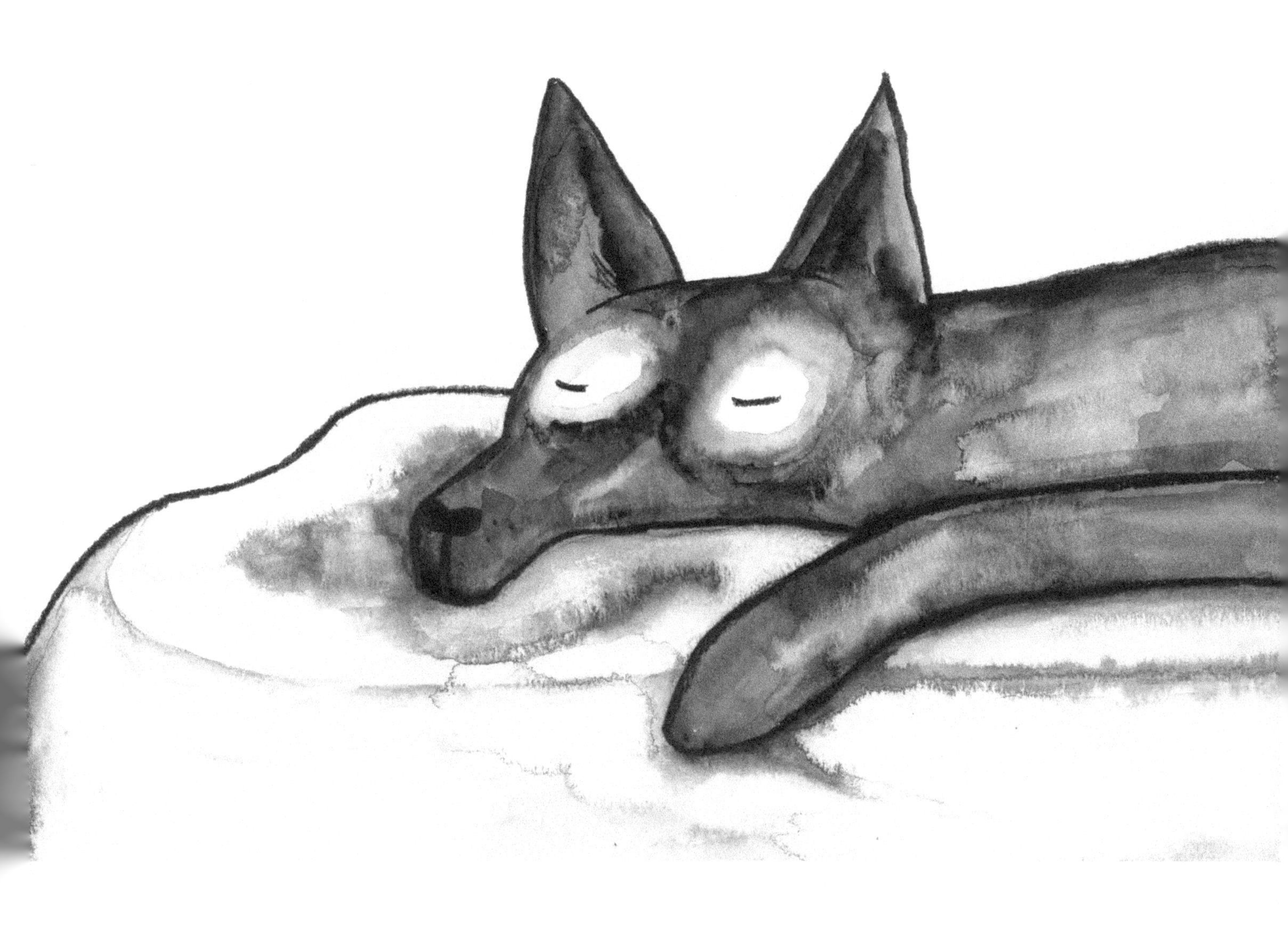

THE END

CPSIA information can be obtained
at www.ICGtesting.com
Printed in the USA
LVHW07s1030221018
594371LV00010B/228/P

9 781546 258759